Give a Goat

Jan West Schrock

Illustrated by Aileen Darragh

I never thought my class would do anything special.
We're just regular fifth graders. But I was wrong!
Here's what happened at our school:

Everyone in our room was restless because of all the rain.

Mrs. Rowell knew we needed a story. She grabbed a book off the shelf. It was *Beatrice's Goat*.

The story was about
a real-life girl named
Beatrice who lived in Uganda,
a country in Africa.

Beatrice wanted to go to school, but
her family couldn't afford to send her.

One day people from far away came to the village and gave Beatrice's mother a goat. Because of that goat, Beatrice's whole life changed. It got better.

The goat gave lots of milk—more than enough for the whole family to drink. Beatrice was in charge of selling the extra milk. With all that milk, Beatrice's family got healthier, and they earned enough money to pay for school. Beatrice finally got her wish!

When Mrs. Rowell finished reading and closed the book, everyone in class seemed to have the same idea. We all shouted: "We want to give a goat!"

Mrs. Rowell looked at us. Then she got a funny smile on her face. She said, "Helping other people takes a lot of planning. And you will have to work together." She gave us kind of a stern look when she said that last bit. "Are you ready to work together?"

Later, my friend Ralph and I went to the library. Miss Bassinger, our librarian, knew all about *Beatrice's Goat* and told us "the goat people" were from Heifer International. She offered to helped us find their website. But Ralph figured it out fast on his own. He's almost a genius with computers.

After reading the Heifer home page, we clicked on the "Get Involved" section and discovered you can send money to buy animals—all kinds of animals—to help people. We weren't just talking about goats, either. They had animals to fit every budget—from ducks to llamas to water buffalo (for the big spenders).

Then we read about something called "passing on the gift." Once a family's goat or duck or water buffalo has a baby, Heifer asks the family to give the baby to a neighbor, so a new family can have a better life. One gift leads to another and another and another, all for the price of one animal. Cool!

The next day on the playground, Ralph and I explained to our classmates how we could give a goat to a family. Everyone—yes, every one of us—liked the idea. After recess we told Mrs. Rowell about the decision. We also told her our whole class wanted to raise $120, enough to buy a goat.

I had a hard time imagining how we would make that much money. But I didn't say so to anyone.

Mrs. Rowell got that funny look on her face again when she heard how serious we were. "We have a math unit coming up," she said. "Maybe we could set up a store here in our school and sell something. But what?"

Ralph spoke up right away, as usual. "Let's sell things teachers want to buy."

"Okay, but what do teachers like?"

We argued about this for a while. Kathy finally got everyone's attention. "They like to eat!" We all laughed.

"Yeah," Ralph added, "teachers are always looking for food. Cookies, candy bars, sodas, anything."

"Okay, maybe so, but how about selling us something that is actually good for us?" suggested Mrs. Rowell.

Alissa started waving her arms. "Healthy snacks! How about healthy snacks?"
Alissa is pretty well known for her granola bars. Most of us really like
it when she shares them. We started
nodding to each other. We agreed
healthy snacks would be good.
We decided to buy nuts and popcorn
and raisins in bulk.

Then the real work began.

Mrs. Rowell loaned us fifteen dollars to get started. Because it was only a loan and not a gift, we knew we would have to pay her back once we made some money.

Mrs. Rowell purchased big bags of nuts, popcorn, and raisins. We divided the food into equal small packages and settled on what to charge. Obviously we had to figure out prices that added up to more than what we had paid to begin with—or we wouldn't make a profit.

Give a Goat | Income | Expense

-15.00

Mrs Rowell

Sales

To run our store right, we had to keep records. Mrs. Rowell also taught us about quality control, inventory, investment, and profit margin. Whew! We were learning a lot.

I loved using the special ledger paper to keep track of everything.

We put the snack packages on the table
in the teachers' lounge with a big sign saying:

"BUY A HEALTHY SNACK SO WE CAN GIVE A GOAT."

The teachers thought the sign was a little strange until we told them about
our math project and what we wanted to do with the money we earned.
Then they all got funny looks on their faces and started buying.

After a while we "broadened our market," as Mrs. Rowell would say, by also selling to kids during our recess periods.

One weekend we sold our snacks during a basketball game. The parent-teacher-group table was right next to ours. It was loaded with brownies and cookies and cupcakes. But when people heard about our project, they lined up to buy our healthy snacks. Some even gave us a few extra dollars.

By the end of the month, we had paid back Mrs. Rowell's loan and still had a profit of $180! All of it was in the cash box.

We had enough money to buy a goat,
a flock of chickens,
and some ducks.

We weren't going to help one family—it was way better than that— we were going to help three families!

Imagine, a whole bunch of children could go to school because of our math project!

	Income	Expense
Mrs Rowell		
Teacher's Lounge		
Basketball Game		
Recess		-15.00
Donations		

When we gathered to celebrate our success, Kate asked if the animals would fly from a farm here in Maine to someplace like Uganda. Everybody laughed to think about chickens on an airplane.

Ralph actually knew the answer, though. He said sometimes Heifer International buys the animals in the same country where families need them, and sometimes Heifer ships the animals by boat or airplane from another country—but usually in a crate, not on a seat!

Ralph told us that Heifer gives animals to families in our own country, too.

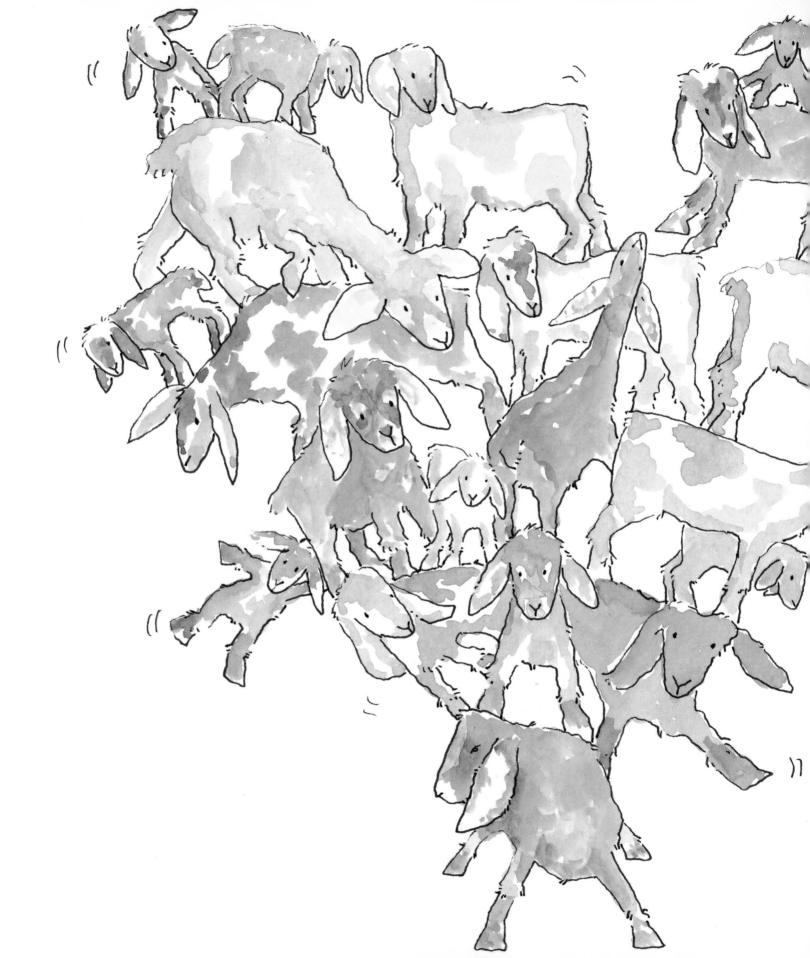

I was surprised and sad to find out that so many families need help.
But I felt good knowing sometimes a little gift can make a big
difference. After all, our class had made a difference for three families
just by selling snacks.

I really liked the idea that if we helped one family,

    they would be able to help another family,

        then another family, and

            then another family,

                in a long chain of passing on the gift.

It turned out other classes at our school wanted to make a difference, too.

Mr. Potter's class organized a Bring-a-Can-to-School Day for the food pantry in town. Mrs. Smith's class held a car wash behind the gym. Her students all got wet, but they raised $150 for the Red Cross.

I think everyone learned that giving—and passing on the gift—feels really good.

FOOD DRIVE DROP OFF

TILBURY HOUSE PUBLISHERS

12 Starr Street, Thomaston, Maine 04861 • 800–582–1899 • www.tilburyhouse.com

First hardcover edition: June 2008
First paperback edition: January 2013
10 9 8 7 6 5 4 3 2

I dedicate this book to children and educators whose neighborhoods reach around the world, and who catch the spirit of giving for a better world. —JWS

To Catherine, Julia, and Elizabeth; and, of course, Matti and her Nubian goat Black Beauty —the model for the pictures in this book. —AD

Library of Congress Cataloging-in-Publication Data

Schrock, Jan West, 1936-
Give a goat / Jan West Schrock ; illustrated by Aileen Darragh. — 1st hardcover ed.
    p. cm.
Summary: After hearing a story about a girl in Uganda whose life is changed for the better by the gift of a goat, a class of fifth-graders pulls together to raise funds to make a similar donation to someone in need.
  ISBN 978-0-88448-301-4 (hardcover : alk. paper)
  [1. Charity—Fiction. 2. Moneymaking projects—Fiction. 3. Schools—Fiction. 4. Cooperativeness—Fiction.]
  I. Darragh, Aileen, 1962- ill. II. Title.
  PZ7.S37938Giv 2008
  [Fic]—dc22   2007043221

Designed by Geraldine Millham, Westport, Massachusetts
Printed in Malaysia by Times Offset (M) Sdn. Bhd. through Four Colour Print Group, Louisville, Kentucky (April 2015) 54081-0

For information about Heifer International, please visit www.heifer.org. For information about Read to Feed, a Heifer International reading incentive, global education, and service learning program, please visit www.readtofeed.org.

Please see www.tilburyhouse.com and click on *Give a Goat* for a variety of ways you can help make a difference, and for suggestions for using this book in the classroom.